Someone's WATCHING
Someone's WAITING

Jamila Gavin

ILLUSTRATED BY
ANTHONY LEWIS

mammoth

To Stroud District Museum
who showed me my first mourning doll
J.G.

For Shirley and David
A.L.

First published in Great Britain in 1998 by Mammoth
an imprint of Egmont Children's Books Limited
Michelin House, 81 Fulham Road, London SW3 6RB

Text copyright © 1998 Jamila Gavin
Illustrations copyright © 1998 Anthony Lewis

The rights of Jamila Gavin and Anthony Lewis
to be identified as the author and illustrator of this work
have been asserted by them in accordance with the
Copyright, Designs and Patents Act 1988

ISBN 0 7497 3106 0

10 9 8 7 6 5 4 3

A CIP catalogue record for this book is
available from the British Library

Printed in Great Britain by Cox & Wyman Ltd,
Reading, Berkshire

Contents

1 The mourning doll

I have taken locks of your chestnut hair,

Live for ever my darling girl;

And the dress of lace we christened you in,

We'll never forget, my precious one.

The satin shoes I embroidered myself

And the gloves of lace to cover your hands.

These things I have taken for remembrance

So that you will live for ever.

THE WOMAN IN black wept as she sat at her sewing-table, cutting and stitching and padding and shaping. The soft white dress of muslin and lace lay like snow across the black folds of her long dress. All around were little boxes of buttons and ribbons and tapes, and spools of many different coloured reels of cotton and silk.

It took her no more than a week, but a week in which she worked almost day and night – for there was no other task she wanted to perform; no other task which could stop her grief from overflowing her broken heart.

And, while she worked, life carried on in the great house, which had never been more full of people. They moved about so silently in their dark, funeral colours; dark as the shadows which gathered behind the drawn curtains. They had blotted out the day, and only the sparse light of a few flickering candles lit their way from room to room. Everyone talked in lowered voices and the other children were restricted to their nursery, amusing themselves with the dolls' house and the rocking-horse, and games with their tin soldiers on the carpet. Every now and then they thought they heard that high singing voice or that familiar, mischievous chuckle, and they looked at each other, silent with remembering, then continued their game.

At last, her task was complete. The woman in black stood up and stretched. She stretched her hands upwards, her fingers spread out as if reaching for something; as if she would grasp some treasured thing from the heavens and bring it back down to her. Then she picked up her creation, as tenderly as if it were a living babe, and took it downstairs. She smiled for the first time and embraced her other children who came running to greet her and who looked in amazement at what she had made.

She set it carefully on the large oak sideboard, and many wept to see it. But then the woman turned to them brightly and exclaimed, 'I think it's time we drew the curtains and let my daughter be part of the family again.'

The dead child's brothers and sister played with the doll as if she were alive,

then, one by one, they all grew up and moved away.

Elizabeth was the youngest and the last to grow up.

'Don't go! Don't leave me alone,' the doll sister seemed to plead with her. 'Who will I have to play with if you grow up and leave me?'

But Elizabeth did grow up and go away. By the time she came back, she was old, and the doll had been put away and forgotten.

2 Voices and shadows

THERE IS A very old house where, sometimes, the wailing of the wind in the eaves can sound like a woman crying; where a chair moves all by itself across the room; where the rocking-horse suddenly rocks when no one is on it; where the sound of a child's running feet can be heard from somewhere upstairs, and a high voice like a tinkling bell calls out, 'Come and find me!'

Often, on stormy nights, the power lines come down and the electricity goes off. So candles and matches are always to hand. But many a time, a naughty, invisible breath has come up to a still, tall flame and blown it out.

The house is called Cote's Hall. It is a very large house situated at the end of a long avenue of ash. Behind the house, the ordered gardens give way to woods of white beam, oak and beech. They rise steeply until they reach the high moor above, curving like the top of a bald pate.

It is a house with many rooms and stairways and passages and alcoves; there are attics at the top and cellars at the bottom.

Uncle Harry and Aunty Evelyn live there alone now – except for Granny Easter. Uncle Harry and Aunty Evelyn are quite old, and Granny Easter is very, very old, and she is senile. No one understands a thing she says. She rambles on, taking anyone who cares to listen into a strange land where ancient memory supersedes the present, tossing her between all eighty-eight years of her past, but never allowing her to live in the present. She sits and sits in her favourite chair in the living-room window, gazing out across the grass towards the curving boughs of the old copper beech. Sometimes she waves as if she sees someone; and she nods and beckons and opens up her arms in an embrace, but no one else sees what she sees, and they just throw up their eyes sympathetically and  murmur, 'Poor Granny.' Sometimes she just seems to be listening.

It was to this house that Emma came one summer, trying not to be nervous of its gloomy passages and dark corners, its up-and-down stairs and odd levels (so you could often wonder which floor you were on). She tried not to be afraid of her tall-ceilinged bedroom, with its arched windows, whose light was partly obscured by a curtain of ivy on the outside and heavy faded blue velvet curtains on the inside.

 She wondered if she would ever fall asleep in that high, brass-framed bedstead under which dark shadows gathered, waiting for the night.

The first night, her Aunt Evelyn came to tuck her in and laughed, saying, 'Oh, Emma, you look like the princess and the pea lying there so small in such a high bed. I'm sorry your cousins Rachel and Jack won't be coming for the holidays. They've gone down with chicken pox, so you'll have to get along with Tombo.'

Emma wanted to get along with Tombo. He liked climbing trees and making dens and riding bikes, as she did. But he wouldn't let her join him. He had glared at her when they first met, as if it were her fault that the others had gone down with the chicken pox. So he ignored her most of the time, as if he didn't care whether she was there or not.

Emma thought she would have no friend at all, until she met Granny Easter. Emma had been watching Tombo below in the garden. He got his bike out of the shed and pedalled off down the cinder track towards the woods. Even from there she could hear the crunch of his tyres on the cinders, and the warning tinkle of his bell as he charged through the bushes. She sighed with frustration. What a beautiful bike it was. If only he would let her ride it.

Then she heard the voice: 'Coo-ee! Ready!' It was as thin and high as a child's and seemed to come from a great distance.

Emma ran out on to the landing and peered down the dark stairwell. The shadows crowded deep. Emma called tentatively, 'Aunty, is that you?'

'I'm hiding! Come and find me!' the voice came from below.

Emma began to descend the stairs into

the shadows, step by step. She reached the first landing . . . The voice called again. It came from lower down and along a corridor leading off to another wing of the house.

'Hurry up, I've been hiding for ages, please come and find me,' the voice pleaded.

'I'm coming,' murmured Emma tentatively, and followed the length of the corridor.

A sudden rush of wind enveloped her as a door flew open. Emma gasped with shock. A hand gripped her arm and pulled her round. 'There you are! There you are!' quavered an old woman's voice. An ancient face loomed up at her, with dark, hollow eyes which blinked like a nervous owl; thin, hard fingers reached up and squeezed her shoulders and chin and tweaked at her hair. 'I've been hiding for ages and you didn't come. Why won't you play with me?' The old woman examined her closer, touching her jeans and tugging her T-shirt. 'I wanted Emmaline. She likes to play hide-and-seek with me.'

'I'm Emma – not Emmaline – though I suppose it's the same name,' replied Emma, alarmed by the strange old lady. 'I'm staying with Aunty Evelyn for three weeks.'

'No, not Emmaline. Your hair is too red and your skin too pale. Oh dear.' The old woman looked disappointed and withdrew into her room, moaning softly. 'Emmaline is so cruel. She won't play with me. I'm too old, too old.'

Nervously, Emma ran on down the corridor not knowing where she would land up. To her relief, the corridor opened out into a black lobby strewn with boots and anoraks and riding hats. She could see the garden through a side window and she felt better.

A mud-splattered Tombo burst in through the side door.

'Oh!' he gasped at the sight of her. 'It's you.' He tugged off his trainers and anorak and took himself off saying, 'I'm starving!'

'Wait for me!' yelled Emma, running after him.

3 A face in the window

AFTER BREAKFAST, TOMBO went back to his beloved bike in the garden shed. He didn't look too pleased when Emma trailed after him.

'What do you want?' he asked her grumpily, as she watched him get out an oilcan and rags.

'I just want to watch. I love bikes.'

'Well don't get in my way – and don't touch.'

'I won't,' muttered Emma.

Tombo got down on his knees with an

oily rag. He peered into the spokes of the wheels and tenderly cleaned and oiled its intricate parts.

'It's a super bike,' Emma breathed, admiringly.

Tombo ignored her and continued to polish vigorously.

'I've got one at home – but not as good as yours,' she persisted.

Tombo raised his eyebrows but didn't answer.

She longed to ask him if she could have a go.

'There's a good rough bit at the end of the garden. I saw it yesterday. Do you bike there?'

'Yeah,' he brightened a bit. 'But I have to

keep to the track. Best is to go scrambling in the woods.'

'You lucky thing,' sighed Emma enviously. 'I wish I'd brought my bike with me. I love doing wheelies and trying to jump ditches.'

'Huh!' grunted Tombo, as if he didn't believe her.

When he had finished, he propped the bike against the side, pausing to admire his handiwork. 'Right, I'm off. Don't touch, will you!' he commanded, and left.

'No, I won't touch your stupid bike,' muttered Emma crossly.

She wandered miserably out across the grass. She would look for the tree-house in the woods which her mother told her she had made when she and Aunty Evelyn were children. She followed the path round the side of the house and down the cinder track which led to the back, where the gardens spread away into the rough and the woods beyond. She waved at Uncle Harry in the kitchen garden, turning over the soil with a hoe. He waved back and she continued on into the woods.

Shafts of sunlight poured through the

branches; the wood rustled and twitched with the wind and birds and scuttling creatures. The track rose steeply, skirting deep hollows and steep slopes of dense undergrowth. Sometimes she followed other little paths which straggled off independently. Looking up at the torsos of tree trunks, her eyes followed the muscular limbs of branches, which reached outwards and upwards, trying to discover signs of a tree-house.

She was surprised when the wood ended abruptly and she found herself on the slopes of the open common, all lumpy and bumpy with molehills and sharp yellow grass. Scrambling on to a high mound, she gazed with exhilaration at the hills and valleys now exposed to her. There was Cote's Hall, clearly visible with its warm yellow, stone walls, many windows and curved, gabled roofs. From the outside, it looked as upright and straightforward as a doll's house; how strange to think that inside, it was such a warren of rooms and corridors and mysterious corners. She wondered which of the many windows was hers. Her eyes moved up from the ground floor to the first then the second – she paused at the second. Her room was on that floor. She identified a window she was sure was hers. Tombo slept on the third floor – the top floor. She frowned, her eyes narrowed against the bright morning light as she counted the floors once more: one, two, three – and yes – four. She was puzzled. There were only three floors in the house. She supposed this was the attic, even though it had the same gabled windows as the other floors.

After a while, Emma descended the slope, back into the woods. She lost sight of the house until she emerged at the bottom again and entered the cultivated regions of the garden. The windows of the house seemed to be watching her, their panes glinting like eyes.

Someone waved to her from a window. Emma raised her hand to wave back, then let it hang uncertainly. Was the figure in *her* window? She stopped and stared and counted again. The figure waved, beckoning her. Emma walked then ran towards the house. She charged up the stairs and burst into her room. It was empty. She puzzled for some moments. Perhaps she was mistaken; or perhaps it was Tombo who had waved. Perhaps he wanted to play with her after all. Thoughtfully, she wandered out on to the landing. She stood at the bottom of the flight of stairs which led up to the third floor where Tombo's room was. A fierce notice was pinned up: NO ADMITTANCE TO GIRLS BEYOND THIS POINT. She peered up through the gloom to the landing above. A pattering, like bare feet, echoed on the floorboards.

'Tombo?' she called tentatively. There was a low rumbling. A single marble rolled to the top of the stairs; it wobbled on the edge, poised on the rim of gravity; Emma held her breath. It teetered on the top step, then toppled over and came bouncing down, step by step, till it landed at her feet. She picked it up and held it in the palm of her hand. She stared into the depths of the marble and felt drawn into its vortex.

A thin, far-off voice was calling: 'Where are you?' It came from the floor above. She was about to go up the stairs when a louder, firmer voice called to her from below.

'Emma! Emma dear! Where are you? Come on down, I have a job for you.' It was Aunt Evelyn.

Emma popped the marble in her pocket and ran down to the kitchen. She was startled to see Tombo there having a drink.

'Did you want me?' she asked him. 'When I was in the garden I saw you wave to me from my window.'

'Of course I didn't. What would I be doing in your bedroom? Don't be silly.'

'Did you wave from your window then?'

'Nope, I don't have a window on your side,' he retorted.

'Well someone rolled this marble down your stairs to me,' she said, holding it out.

'You haven't been up in my room have you?' he demanded furiously.

'No, I haven't. I thought you waved at me, and I went to look for you, but I didn't go up your silly stairs.'

He glanced at the round, glassy marble lying in the palm of Emma's hand. It gleamed like an eyeball, as brown as a hazelnut, coiling away into darker brown depths, mesmerising him for a moment. Idly, he shrugged. 'Not me. I don't have marbles any more.'

'Oh well,' said Emma, popping it back in her pocket. 'Finders keepers, then.'

'Just stay away from my floor. It's forbidden except with my permission,' muttered Tombo, sinking his teeth into some toast.

4 Granny Easter's doll

AUNTY EVELYN SAID, 'Granny Easter needs her hair brushing, Emma. If you're not doing anything for the moment, would you do it for me?'

Emma looked alarmed. 'Just me?'

Aunty Evelyn didn't seem to notice the anxiety in Emma's voice. 'I'd be so grateful if you would. If it's one thing Granny Easter loves, it's having her hair brushed and played with. So – if you've ever had fantasies about being a hairdresser, now's your chance.'

Aunty Evelyn took her along the dark passageway to Granny Easter's room.

Emma thought it would be a dark, smelly, cluttered, old woman's room, but she had a surprise. It was a warm, generous room with flowery curtains in front of long French windows through which the light poured most of the day. It was full of the prettiest things: little tables, a sideboard crammed with ornaments and photographs, comfortable armchairs, padded footstools, a rocking-chair and a deep sofa. At the far end, standing in an alcove, was a mahogany dressing-table with a three-panelled mirror.

'Hello, Granny Easter,' Aunty Evelyn shouted in a jolly voice because Granny

Easter was deaf. 'I've brought Emma to do your hair today.'

Granny Easter was sitting in an upright chair, looking out on to the garden. She looked different from the wild woman who had accosted Emma earlier. Her face was calm and sweet and as finely wrinkled as the surface of still water. Her deep, dark eyes glowed. She held out both hands and drew Emma to her. Her hands were soft and gentle, not like the steely hands which grabbed Emma this morning.

'Emma, not Emmaline!' murmured Granny Easter to herself sadly. Painfully, the old lady eased herself up out of the armchair, allowing Aunty Evelyn to help her over to the chair in front of the dressing-table.

'Granny had a bad accident when she was a child,' Aunt Evelyn explained quietly. 'She fell down the stairs and broke her leg. It never mended properly. That's why she limps so badly.'

Granny Easter's ancient face appeared in three mirrors – the front and two profiles – while the room receded darkly into the background.

'She didn't want me to grow up,' Granny mumbled.

Emma came and stood behind her, and her face also appeared in all three mirrors. They looked at each other. Aunt Evelyn's image entered the picture and smiled at her through the mirror. 'Don't be put off by any of Granny's fantasies or visions,' she said, quietly reassuring her. 'She sees things we don't – and it's best to go along with it. Just leave when you've done as much as you want,' then, giving Emma a grateful hug, she left her to it.

Granny Easter nodded at Emma through the mirror.

Emma smiled shyly. She ran her fingers through the old lady's hair, pulling out stray pins and shaking out her tight curls. She took up a silver brush and gently pulled it through the thin, grey hair. As she brushed, Emma fell into a rhythm and, for a while both were silent. Granny Easter's eyes closed and a smile fluttered contentedly round her mouth.

Emma's eyes roamed around the room, noting the strange oddments, photographs and bits of china covering all the surfaces.

Reflected through one of the side mirrors, Emma saw the doll. It was propped on top of a corner cabinet, almost lost behind the curtain. Emma stopped brushing. Granny Easter didn't stir. Quietly, Emma laid down the brush and turned round, but she couldn't see the doll. She looked back into the mirror. There it was again, but somehow only visible through the mirror.

It was on the tall walnut cabinet in the far left corner of the room, near the window, but, even when Emma went over and stood on tiptoe, she couldn't see the doll.

Emma checked that Granny Easter was still asleep. She took a footstool and stood on it in front of the cabinet.

There was a flurry of dust, as her fingers made contact with something soft. She pulled gently and the doll came into view.

'Oh!' Emma gave a soft gasp of pleasure.

'You're beautiful.' She lifted the doll into her arms and got down. Deftly, she shook and patted the dust from its clothes and hair, then set the doll on the table in the window.

Normally she was not one to play with dolls, but she had never seen one like this before. She looked so life-like. She stood taller than most dolls, and her long, flowing, creamy muslin dress gleamed like moonlight. Her hands, which rested

36

gently on her skirts, were enclosed in cream lace gloves with a little frill at the wrists, and on her feet were the most delicate cream satin slippers. Hanging from her sash was a small purse with the initials *EEEE* embroidered in fancy curling letters. The doll was beautiful. Long, lustrous, chestnut brown hair fell in twists of curls down her shoulders. It matched the colour of her gleaming, dark brown eyes, which seemed more real than glassy. But it was the face which amazed Emma; it glowed luminous, almost living, with a soft blush heightening the cheeks. The pink lips seemed almost moist, and were slightly parted, as if any minute she would speak.

'Where are you, dear?' Granny Easter's voice quavered. 'Why have you stopped?'

Emma returned quickly and resumed brushing.

Now she could see the doll behind her, reflected in all three mirrors. Shadow and sunlight alternated as clouds swept across the sun. The doll drifted in and out of light and shade – visibility and invisibility. The sun disappeared altogether and the room darkened. All she could see of the doll in the mirror was a white blur.

Emma coiled and pinned Granny's hair, then took a pace back to admire it. From the depths of the room behind her, a face materialised. It came nearer and nearer until it peered over her shoulder. Emma stared back.

In the mirror, the face broke up into dancing reflections, so that Emma couldn't be sure what she was seeing; a cloud, a sunbeam, dark images – or – a little girl's face, with long, dark curls and deep brown eyes? They stared and stared, each daring the other to be the first to look away.

A fierce caw from a crow caused Emma to break the spell. She whirled round. Outside, a shining black bird dived from the top of the old cedar tree. It spun in the air with something in its beak. She leaned forward to see. The crow cawed again and the object fell from its beak and plummeted towards the ground. In a flash, the bird turned and dived, catching the object before it hit the ground. Then it wheeled away.

No one stood behind Emma. Only the doll on the table.

Emma turned back to the mirror. It was shimmering.

Granny Easter opened her eyes, gazing beyond her own reflection. They filled with tears. 'I'm sorry, I'm sorry for growing up. Please forgive me.'

Emma stood perfectly still. 'I hope you don't mind, Granny, I took down your doll to look at it.'

The silence imprisoned them. Granny Easter's eyes had closed again, a tear still trapped in the wrinkle of her cheek. Emma felt suffocated by the silence. All she could hear was the thumping of her own heart. Then, gradually, the outside world seemed to come alive again; she heard the clock ticking and the birds twittering outside; she heard the urgent caw of the crow as it returned to the branches of the cedar.

Through the window, she glimpsed Tombo racing down the cinder track on the far side of the lawn. How she wished she could have joined him. She turned towards the doll. It seemed to be waiting for her, its hands outstretched. Emma took them in hers and, lifting her down to the carpet, very quietly began to play.

In the middle of that night, Emma awoke. She had been dreaming about the doll. An all-night lamp on the stable roof cast a dim light into her bedroom, creating menacing shapes which crawled around the walls and across the ceiling. The long bending and twisting shapes of the magnolia tree outside her window moved and tossed, tipping her room like a boat.

For a while, she felt her homesickness was as deep as the sea and would drown her. At last, she rolled over on to her back, staring into the shifting darkness.

Her brain was already flickering with dreams when, through her half-closed eyes, real or unreal, she saw a shape taking form. It wavered into view like a slowly developing photograph; a lady wearing a long black skirt and black fitted jacket. On the lapel was a black and silver brooch, and round her paper white throat was a string of jet beads. Her hands were covered in black gloves and on her head she wore a broad-brimmed black hat with a black lacy veil, through which her face gleamed like a pale moon drifting behind dark clouds. She sat on a ledge in the window, softly moaning like a low wind.

Emma struggled on to her elbows. 'Aunty? Is that you? Is something wrong?'

The figure rose and glided noiselessly towards her. Emma tried to speak, but no sound came from her mouth. The lady in black stretched out a hand as if in greeting.

Emma saw moonlight glint on steel. A pair of long, sharp scissors gleamed in the black-gloved hand which reached for a lock of her hair.

5 The fourth floor

THE WEATHER TURNED horrible. It rained and rained for days. Tombo skulked around, unable to ride his bike. He chummed up with boys in the village, sometimes going to their houses to watch television or play video games; or he just kept to himself in his room, only emerging at meal-times. He hardly looked at Emma. It was as though she was invisible.

So Emma went to Granny Easter. She was no longer afraid of her old age, nor her jumbled-up memories. Granny Easter liked Emma to play – though she often behaved as if there was another child there – a child she called Emmaline. Granny would smile and wave at her. And when Emma finished doing Granny's hair, Granny would say, 'Let's play,' and she would set out the Chinese Chequers or a game for three players. She would deal and play, trump and lose, excitedly crying, 'Oh, you are cunning!' or, 'I beat you that time, Emmaline!'

Other times, Granny would curl her arms around her knees and rock, miserably wailing, 'I'm sorry, I'm sorry. I couldn't help growing up. Why won't you forgive me?' and Emma would creep away puzzled and saddened by the grief which overwhelmed the old lady.

But, most of all, it was the doll that Emma looked forward to playing with. She spoke softly to her as if she were alive. 'You are the only doll I've ever liked. I love your hair. It's so real,' she marvelled as she brushed out its long soft, lustrous curls. Sometimes she plaited it with ribbons, or coiled and pinned it up, experimenting with all sorts of different styles. She wondered about the four Es embroidered on the doll's purse. 'Are you an Emma like me? Or Elsie? Ethel? Elizabeth? Ernestina? Or are you Emmaline who Granny sees? I'll call you Emmaline – so we are Emma and Emmaline. Will you be my best friend, Emmaline?' Emma was startled that day, when Granny Easter, whom she thought was asleep, murmured, 'Yes, dear! Be her friend. Emmaline was so cross with me when I grew up.'

The rain stopped and the lawns and gardens dried once more under the hot sun. 'Come on!' cried Emma, picking up Emmaline. 'Let's go out into the garden.' Granny Easter was dozing when Emma quietly opened the French windows in Granny Easter's room. She crept into the garden and crept away with Emmaline held tenderly in her arms.

Tombo was racing around on his bike, doing jumps and wheelies.

'If only, if only Tombo would let me ride it . . .' Emma sighed into the doll's ear with envy and longing. 'He's so mean, it's a good thing you're my friend, otherwise I'd be very lonely. But I wish he'd play with me.' She stood wistfully as Tombo raced passed her without even a glance. She turned to Emmaline. 'Did anyone ever show you the tree-house? Let's find it. It could be our own little home.' She set off towards the woods.

Crossing the cinder track past the vegetable garden, Emma glanced up at the windows of the house. She stopped, puzzled and amazed. Exactly as before, someone waved from her bedroom window. This time she knew it couldn't be Tombo, for there he was cycling through the bushes.

'Who's waving to me from my bedroom window?' she muttered into the doll's hair. 'It's not Tombo, Aunty Evelyn's in town, and it's not Uncle Harry. Shall we go and see?'

Forgetting about the tree-house, she tucked Emmaline under her arm and ran indoors.

By the time she got to her room it was empty. Somewhere above, from a great distance, a voice called sweetly, 'Emmaline! Emmaline!'

'Someone's calling you, surely it can't be Granny,' Emma told the doll. She wandered to the bottom of Tombo's stairs and stared up into the forbidden territory. 'I'm not allowed up there. It's Tombo's floor.'

Emma looked at the doll. Emmaline's eyes seemed to speak to her, pleading with her: Take me upstairs, take me upstairs.

Feeling like a thief, she tiptoed up the

stairs to the landing of the third floor. Her back tingled, excited by her wickedness. On Tombo's door hung another notice: ENTER AT YOUR PERIL. HUNGRY LIONS.

'Aren't boys silly?' giggled Emma. But the silence made her nervous. She was about to creep down, when she heard a voice again, calling urgently.

'Emmaline!' The voice didn't come from downstairs, but from above her. Emma turned, startled.

'Tombo? Is that you?'

Emma swung open Tombo's door. No Tombo. No hungry lions. Just the chaos of his unmade bed and his clothes all over the floor and his books and comics strewn as though a tornado had torn

through his room. She shut the door.

The voice called again – a woman's voice, so soft, so warm. It came from even higher. 'Emmaline!'

Emma looked around the landing. There were no more up flights of stairs. This was the top of the house.

She saw a thick velvet curtain. It moved almost imperceptibly, as if a faint draught blew from behind. Emma went forward cautiously and drew it aside. There was a door. She looked at it questioningly. Her hand hesitated for a second then she gripped the doorknob and opened it towards her.

It was like stepping outside. She recoiled briefly as a cold wind blew into her face. There was yet another flight of stairs. *Another floor.* So there *was* a fourth floor. Emma began to climb.

At the top of the landing she found a small landing and a door. She reached out to open it, then held back. She shivered, unsure. A feeling of dread curled up her back. She didn't want to open the door. She looked at Emmaline. A small smile hovered over the doll's mouth; her eyes brimmed dark, but shining, in the gloom. Go on, open it! she seemed to say.

As if commanded, Emma obeyed.

A long, narrow room stretched before her, with a low pitched roof held up by beams. At the far end, in the window, was a sewing-table covered in reels of cotton, needles, pin-cushions and scraps of material. Before it sat the figure of the woman in black. She didn't turn as Emma entered, but moaned softly as she sewed.

'Excuse me?' Emma stepped forward
shyly.

The figure didn't move or answer. Emma
came closer. She stretched out a hand to
touch her arm but made no contact. Solid
dissolved into light and air; shadows into
reflections. 'Hello?'

The woman came forward, smiling
through tears.

'I didn't know there was anyone else in

the house,' Emma murmured.

'Ah!' said the lady, her voice was low with deep sadness. 'I'm glad you've come and brought Emmaline.'

'Are you a visitor like me?' asked Emma, looking at the woman's old-fashioned, long, black skirt and high-throated blouse.

'Let me measure you,' said the mysterious woman, not answering Emma's question. She held out a measuring-tape.

Emma set down the doll and dutifully stood with her arms akimbo as the woman measured her height and waist, shoulders, neck and arms.

'What a perfect playmate you'll make for my little Emmaline,' breathed the lady in black. 'Stand still while I pin your blouse.

You will stay with me now, won't you? For ever . . . for ever and ever . . .' The words rose and fell . . . Emma heard them through a roaring in her ears as if she stood under a waterfall . . . *For ever and ever and ever . . .*

Emma felt slivers of cold air on her neck as the woman moved behind her. She heard sobbing mixed with the sound of snipping and clipping. 'I need a lock of your hair, a snip of your blouse and a piece from your trousers.'

Emma felt weak with dizzy fear. Her eyes blurred, the room swam and tipped. She reached for the doll. 'Emmaline, what's happening?'

Then, as if from a great distance, she heard a voice of reproof. 'Really, Emma! It's very naughty of you to be up here. Come down immediately.' A hand gripped hers and tugged her through the door.

As she hurtled down the stairs, she thought a voice wailed behind her, 'Don't go. Don't leave me!'

The grip on her arm loosened. Her limbs came back to life again. She found herself crouching outside her own room with Emmaline clutched in her arms. She was free.

Emma felt someone watching her. She raised her eyes fearfully. It was Granny Easter slumped in a chair on the lower landing.

'Granny?' said Emma softly, going over to her. 'Are you all right?'

Granny Easter's eyes flew open. Her hand reached out and gripped Emma's arm. 'Don't go up to the fourth floor ever again. *Ever*,' she whispered harshly.

6 Friends at last?

'**E**MMA! AUNT EVELYN wants me to show you the tree-house.' Tombo stood in the doorway of Granny Easter's room.

His resentful voice disturbed the hushed atmosphere and Granny Easter, who had been dozing, stirred and fretted in her dreams. 'Emmaline, don't be so unkind.'

Emma, who was sprawled on the carpet playing with the doll, got to her knees, hardly believing her ears.

'Well? Are you coming or not?' demanded Tombo.

'Oh yes, yes!' cried Emma joyfully, 'I'm coming. Let me just put Emmaline back on top of the cabinet.'

'Who's Emmaline?' Tombo asked curiously.

'Oh, just a doll,' said Emma, pulling the stool over to the cabinet. 'She lives up here. I found her,' and with less care than usual she ignored Emmaline's look of fury and pushed her back into the dusty darkness.

The rain had passed now, and it was warm and bursting with sunshine. All that day and the next, Emma roamed through the woods with Tombo. He showed her the tree-house which could only be entered by way of the rope ladder, and the swing which Uncle Harry had hoisted from a high branch; they damned the stream which gushed down the hillside to create pools to splash about in. Emma was sure Tombo enjoyed her company, though he made a point of frowning most of the time. But once, when she tried to jump over the stream and landed with a splosh right in the middle, he roared with laughter.

'Tombo,' Emma asked him while they lay half-drowned in a field of long grass, chewing on a cocksfoot stem and watching the scabious and cornflower nodding purple and blue above their noses, 'who's the woman living up on the fourth floor?'

'Don't be daft,' laughed Tombo. 'There is no fourth floor.'

'But I've counted four,' insisted Emma. 'Twice now. I'll show you.'

'Look, Emma,' growled Tombo impatiently, 'I have been coming to Cote's Hall for years and I always have the room at the top of the house, so I should know. There are only three floors. Mind you, Uncle Harry told me that when Granny Easter was a child there was a fourth floor, but her father had it removed.'

'Completely removed?' Emma rolled over

and sat up, hugging her knees to her chest.

'Where did I go then?' Emma struggled with confusion. 'I went up to the third floor, but there was another door and another flight of stairs and . . .'

Tombo sat up furiously. 'You what? Have you been up to my floor? How dare you! Can't you read? It's private up there. I never let anyone go without my permission.' He leapt to his feet and strode away.

'But, Tombo . . . please listen . . . I didn't go in your room . . . honestly. I was just exploring. I heard a voice calling . . . and then there was that marble . . . someone rolled it down . . . Oh please come back . . . it was awful up there . . . there was this woman . . .'

But Tombo didn't look back. He went to the shed, got out his bike and cycled off.

Emma wandered back to the kitchen and found Aunty Evelyn preparing lunch.

'How many floors does this house have?' asked Emma.

'Three floors, dear. You're on the second and Tombo's on the third – the top floor.'

'But I . . .' Emma, hesitated.

Aunty Evelyn turned and noticed Emma's pale face. 'Are you all right, dear? Not sickening for something, I hope. I'm so glad you and Tombo have started to get along at last.'

'Yes, Aunty,' murmured Emma listlessly.

'And what on earth have you been doing

to your hair?' exclaimed Aunt Evelyn. 'You haven't tried to cut it yourself have you? It's all ragged and uneven. Oh dear. I don't have time to sort it out now. I'll try and tidy it up later. What would your mother say?'

'No, I didn't cut it. I'm trying to grow it,' said Emma, feeling the ends of her hair. 'It never seems to get any longer. I think I'd better go and see Granny Easter. I haven't been for a few days.' Emma paused in the doorway. 'Aunty, did Granny Easter have a sister?'

'Oh yes. Granny Easter has three brothers and a sister called Emmaline who died unfortunately.'

It was with a sense of foreboding that Emma quietly opened Granny Easter's door. The old lady was sitting in her winged armchair in the French windows. Her head lolled as she slept. Emma sat on the stool at her feet and touched her knee gently. 'Granny,' she said softly. 'Granny, why did you tell me not to go up to the fourth floor when there isn't a fourth floor?'

'Emmaline!' Granny mumbled. 'Poor Emmaline. It was all my fault. I should have watched her. Now she watches me. She wanted me to stay with her, even pushed me down the stairs – the naughty girl. She hates me for growing up. Now she watches you and wants you . . .' Granny's voice trailed away into sleep . . . 'always watching and wanting and waiting . . .'

Emma glanced up at the cabinet and then quickly away again. She didn't want to see the doll today. She hoped Tombo might forgive her and let her play with him once more.

Then Emma caught Emmaline's marble gaze in the mirror. The doll's deep glassy eyes looked down at her from the top of the cabinet. Emma heard her high, sharp voice say inside her head, 'Where have you been? Why did you leave me? I've been lonely without you. You're not going are you? Please play with me . . . please Emmie!'

With a sigh, Emma took the footstool and reached up for the doll. 'I'm sorry I haven't played with you for a day or two,' Emma apologised. 'Tombo and I went exploring in the woods. It was such fun and I thought he would be my friend, until I told him I'd been up on the fourth floor. Then he was furious. I don't think he'll ever talk to me again.' Tears came into

Emma's eyes as she propped Emmaline into the cushions on the sofa.

Emmaline looked unsympathetic. 'You're *my* friend,' her jealous eyes exclaimed. 'I've waited such a long time for someone to play with. You shouldn't have gone off with him.'

'Tombo told me about the fourth floor,' whispered Emma. 'There used to be one, but not any more. It was pulled down.'

'Oh, but there is.' The doll's eyes glimmered. 'You know there is. We went there together, didn't we? Let's go now. I'll show you.'

There was such force behind Emmaline's desire, that Emma was compelled to obey even though she felt afraid. She carried her to the third floor. Emma no longer thought about Tombo, or how angry he would be, and when she heard the soft, motherly voice calling, 'Emmaline! Come to me, darling!' there was no choice but to open the door behind the blue curtain and carry the doll on upwards, up into the chill of the stairway which led to the fourth floor.

Emma was filled with dread. She opened the door. The long, beamed room spread before her on and on as if it went on for ever into a blinding brightness. From a great distance, she saw the woman in black sitting at the sewing-table in the arched window. At her side was a child all in white, who stood patiently while the woman dressed a doll.

The doll's hair was reddish brown, glistening, real and cut to a bob with a fringe. Its marble eyes were light brown like hazelnuts and the finest cotton had been chosen for its pale, freckled skin. The woman tucked and pinned a T-shirt embroidered with the letter E. Then she slipped on a pair of rough, blue denim jeans and fitted a pair of trainers on the doll's feet.

The woman called to Emma. 'Come

and play with my little girl. She's so lonely.'

The girl in white turned, smiling, and held out her hands. 'Mama promised to find me someone to play with.' She took the Emmaline doll from Emma's arms and stood it next to the new doll. 'I like you. Look what we've been making, Mama and I.'

Fearfully, Emma looked at the newly made doll. It had got her clothes, her hair, her face. Emma stepped back with dread. She rushed to the door and flung it open, but there was nothing on the other side. Nothing but a black, fathomless void.

'Oh, you mustn't go,' said the little girl. 'There's no need for you to grow up. No need at all. I'm never going to let you go.'

Never, never, never. The words roared in Emma's ears, like blood pumping furiously.

Never, never, never . . . She stumbled across the room to the window. She could see the garden below. She laughed and cried, 'There's Tombo!' He was cycling down the cinder track. Desperately, she pushed open the window and leant out.

'Tombo! Tombo!' she screamed. 'There *is* a fourth floor. Look up and see me! I'm sorry I went up to your floor. Please forgive me. I only wanted to play with you. Wait!'

7 A girl in white

TOMBO LAUGHED WITH exhilaration. How fast he rode, and with no effort at all, so fast, so silent; his bike hardly seemed to touch the ground; there was no crunch of tyres on the gravel, no sound of whirring wheels. Riding behind him was a girl in white.

'Where are you going?' she asked.

'To the churchyard,' shouted Tombo, 'it's a great place for wheelies and jumps. Just don't tell anyone we've been there. I'm not allowed.'

'I won't tell. Never!' screamed the girl.

Emma leant even further out of the window. She saw Tombo strobing in and out of the light and shade between the high hedges and the avenue of trees.

As they streaked past, the girl looked up at Emma in the window with jealous eyes, and waved. Then they were gone.

'Tombo! Come back!' Emma screamed as he vanished from her sight.

They weaved, dangerously sharp, tipping

at such steep angles that, sometimes, he had to put his foot to the ground to steady the bike. They bounced and flew over the grassy mounds of ancient graves, twisting among stone monuments and towering angels.

It was an ancient graveyard with monuments and statues and mossy head-stones engraved in Latin and old English going back and back in time; and there were so many that the humps of old graves, whose stones had long gone, nudged side by side with newer graves and their freshly chiselled inscriptions.

'Yahoo!' he yelled like a cowboy as he rode the machine, bucking like a bronco, rearing up the bike and leaping obstacles, the engine at full throttle. The bike flew through the air. For a moment, it seemed suspended; hanging in the air as if it could thrust upwards into space. But it didn't.

There was a yell and a crunch and it plunged down, all spokes and spinning tyres. Tombo lay winded, sprawling across a grave with his legs all twisted.

A white-gloved hand rested briefly on the bark of a tree. Then was gone.

★ ★ ★

From the fourth floor of Cote's Hall came
a long, high-pitched scream which sent the
rooks scattering upwards into the dazzling
sky. A scream so high, that it could have
been a distant rabbit caught in the talons of
a hawk.

Someone heaved up the bike and leant it
against a tombstone. Tombo looked up
dazed. He saw a pair of denim-clad legs
and a white T-shirt. The sun was caught in

her red hair. 'Emma?'

She indicated that she could cycle home and get help.

Tombo half-fainted. 'Not likely! Leave my bike alone. I'll manage.' He spoke with such contempt that she turned her back and walked away.

Tombo groaned and grasped his leg. Gripping the tombstone, he dragged himself to his feet and tried to reach for the bike, but fell on to his hands and knees, crippled by the searing pain when his foot made contact with the ground.

'Emma!' he yelled in defeat. 'Come back!'

She came back.

He leant against the tombstone of his ancestor. It wasn't a big one. It was a child's grave with a stone cherub praying on a pedestal over the chiselled inscription which read:

Suffer the little ones to come unto me.
Our most precious
Emmaline Edith Elizabeth Easter
born 17 June 1908
taken from us to live in heaven
on 7 September 1917

'Help me on,' he begged. 'You could wheel me back.'

She brought the bike closer. With a shout

of pain, Tombo eased himself on to the seat. Then, clasping the handlebars, she guided the bike in and out of the tombs and mounds. His head lolled against her back. She was solid yet not solid. Strange sensations and images streamed through his brain – yet no sound. It was as if his ears were blocked with cotton-wool. Emma had not spoken one word since she came to help him.

And still she spoke not one word as they wound in and out of the humps and bumps and on to the path, which ran through the gate out of the graveyard and back into the garden.

'Hey, Emma,' Tombo beseeched her as they approached the house. 'Don't tell anyone I was riding in the graveyard. Uncle Harry will confiscate my bike if he hears. Just say I fell off in the garden. Will you? Please? I'll let you ride my bike whenever you want.'

She sighed as if she was air.

A hushed cluster of people, some kneeling, some standing, encircled someone lying on the gravel in front of the house. Tombo slid off the bike and heard it fall to the ground behind him.

His aunt hurried up, her face distorted with horror. She embraced him and tried to lead him away.

'What's happened? What?' The pain seared through his leg as he tried to see who lay on the ground. He caught sight of outstretched fingers and a doll lying nearby, dressed in T-shirt and jeans, with red hair, just like Emma.

Granny Easter leant on her stick. Stricken words sobbed from her lips. 'My fault. My fault.'

They said Emma had fallen from her bedroom window.

Those who were old enough remembered a past tragedy. When Granny Easter was a child, she and her brothers and sister loved playing up on the fourth floor, though they weren't supposed to. One day, Granny's little sister Emmaline fell out of the fourth floor window and was killed. She was the favourite, and it broke her mother's heart. Within two years the mother had died too. Granny Easter's father was so upset, he had the fourth floor removed.

Now it had happened again. No one knew where the doll came from – a doll which looked like Emma.

At her funeral, they put the doll into the coffin with Emma. As the first clods of earth were shovelled into the grave, Granny Easter hobbled forward carrying another doll. A beautiful doll in a long, white dress, with dark, lustrous curls and brown eyes. She tossed the doll into the grave. 'Poor Emmaline. She just wanted someone to play with.'

These days, Granny Easter sits in her rocking-chair and rocks and rocks. It is Tombo now, who goes to visit her when he comes to Cote's Hall. Granny Easter is the only one who understands when he tells her what had happened in the graveyard.

'Watch them play, dear,' she says comfortingly. And Tombo sees two little girls playing with their dolls, one an old, fashioned doll in a long, white dress, and the other, a modern doll in jeans and a T-shirt.

Sometimes, Tombo stands on the third floor landing outside his bedroom and hears a low moaning voice:

> *I have taken locks of your chestnut hair,*
> *Live for ever my darling girl;*
> *And the dress of lace we christened you in,*
> *We'll never forget, my precious one.*
> *The satin shoes I embroidered myself*
> *And the gloves of lace to cover your hands.*
> *These things I have taken for remembrance*
> *So that you will live for ever.*

91

Sometimes on the third floor landing he sees the blue velvet curtain billow slightly, but he never, never goes to see if there are stairs behind, leading up to a fourth floor.

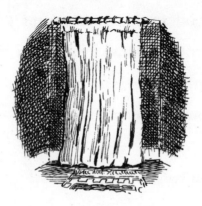